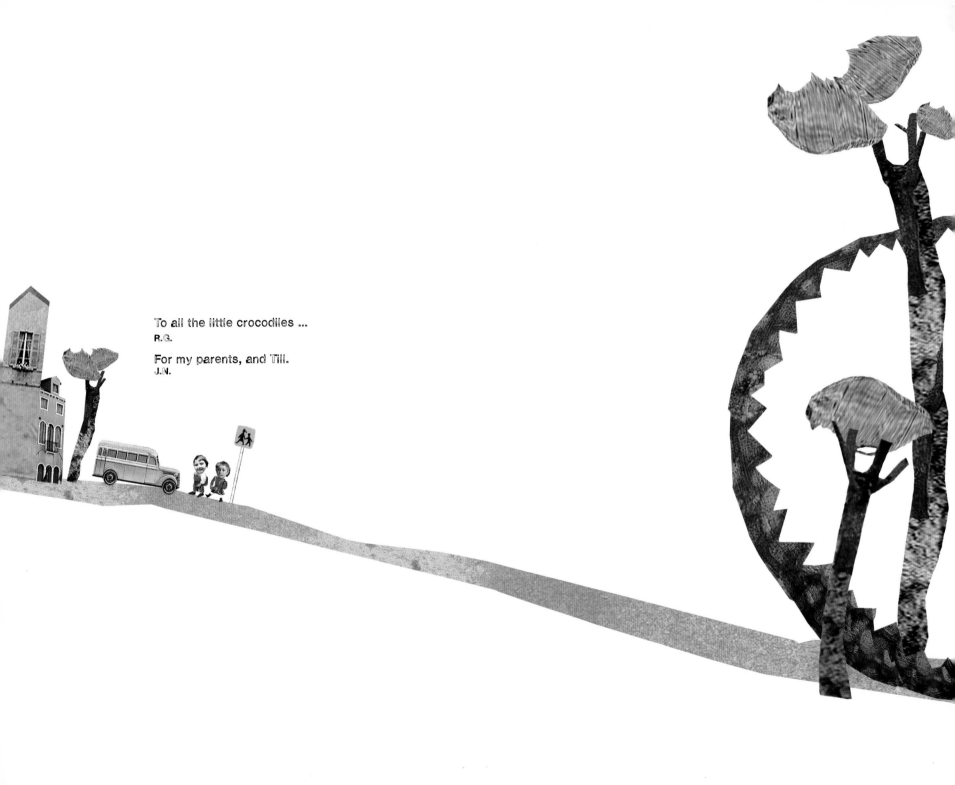

To all the little crocodiles ...
R.G.

For my parents, and Till.
J.N.

I am IVAN Crocodile!

René Gouichoux
Julia Neuhaus

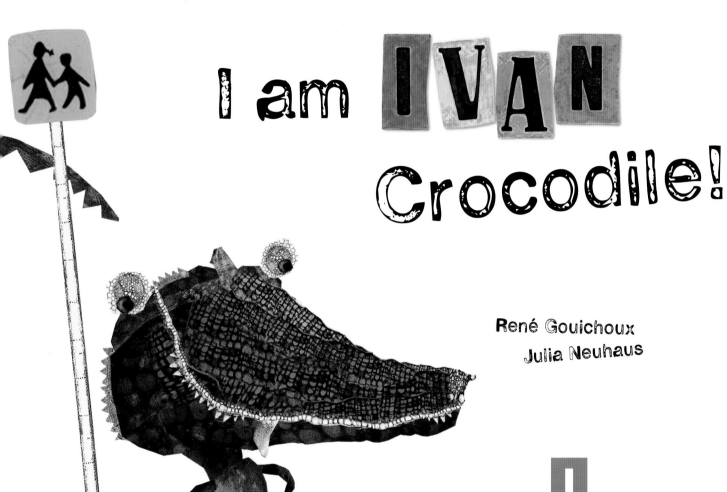

BERBAY
PUBLISHING

My name is Ivan.

I am six years old and I am a **C**rocodile.

I look like a boy
but, inside, I am a crocodile.
It's not something you can see, of course,
because it's inside.

I don't go around baring my long teeth, scaring people.
That's because I'm **n**ice.
Maybe too nice.
That's what the teacher says.

Sometimes, in the schoolyard, the others form a circle around me.

They bump into me and yell things in my ears.

"Hey, Crazy!" they shout.

They take it in turns to push me and spin me around.

They laugh out loud, and I laugh too.

For a bit of fun, I start chasing them.

But their yelling just gets louder and louder.

It's too Loud!

I remember what happened one hot summer's day.
It was really hot, a real CrOCOdile summer!

I was walking in the schoolyard and, as I walked, I licked my lips.
My tongue was going from left to right, right to left.

The others probably thought I was hungry and wanted to eat them.
But I didn't want to eat them, I promise!

It was just that I was hot, and that's what we crocodiles do when we're hot –
we lick our lips, tongue going
left to right, right to left.

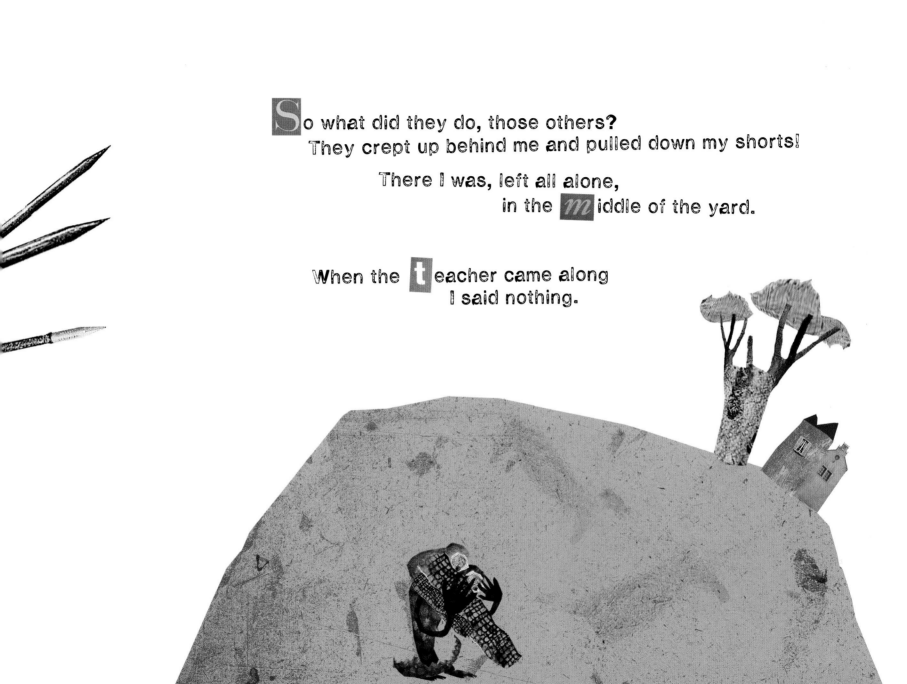

So what did they do, those others?
They crept up behind me and pulled down my shorts!

There I was, left all alone,
in the middle of the yard.

When the teacher came along
I said nothing.

I could have bitten them,
I could have sunk my teeth into them,
I could have torn them to pieces
with my crocodile teeth!

"**Oh**! Ivan, Ivan,
what have they done to you?"
cried the teacher, taking me in her arms.

My teacher smells nice, like my mum.
I like my teacher.

She always speaks softly to me, so softly.

I snapped my **c**rocodile teeth snap snap
and I looked up at her, stretching my crocodile body.
I wanted her to see that I was very strong
but that I meant no harm.

"Yes, I know," said the teacher,
cradling me gently in her arms.

"Calm down, Ivan" she whispered,
slowly stroking my back.

Behind us, the others were pulling faces,
making fun of me.
The teacher couldn't see them.

I opened my eyes wide and
snapped my teeth

snap
snap

to show them I was a crocodile
and to let them know
if they came any closer ...

The teacher kept saying "Calm down, Ivan.
Stop it, Ivan, please."
She rubbed my back, saying over and over, "Shh, shh, it's all right."

Behind us, the others kept moving closer.
I let out a loud **Hahahaha !**

"Shh, Ivan, don't be silly!"

The Others were all around us, laughing.
They put fingers to the sides of their heads and made circles with
their hands. They think I don't know what that means, but I do.

It means crazy.

I'm not crazy,
I'm a crocodile.

It's not the same thing!

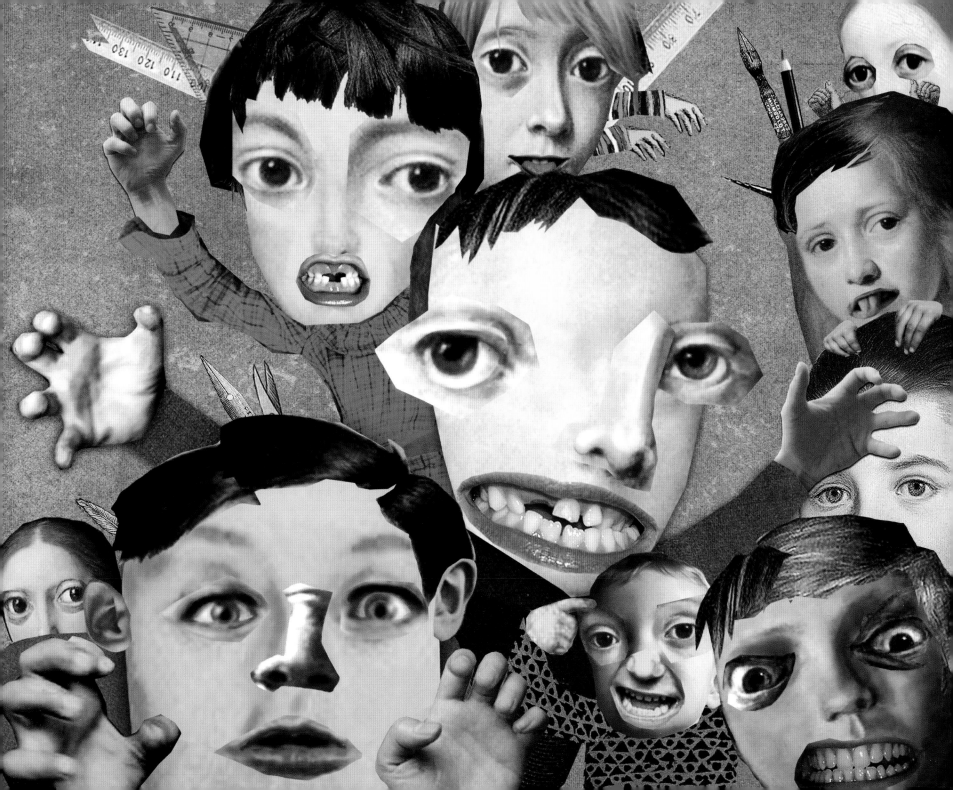

When I go home after school, carrying my schoolbag,
I'm glad I haven't eaten anybody.
I've been nice, like mum told me.

I'm so happy I just have to shout
as I walk along the street.

With my shirt hanging out of my pants
I make some of my crocodile moves.
That's how I show the others that
I could have eaten them, but didn't.

They call me from the other side of the street,
"**Hey, Crazy!**"
I make a sign with my hand, and they make the sign too.
It's the sign they make in the schoolyard,
fingers to the side of their heads.
It makes them laugh.

I do a **b**it of a crocodile waddle,
just enough to show them that if I wanted to ...

Anyway, Crazy is a good name
for a crocodile.
Crazy the **crocodile.**

At home, of course,
Mum knows, and so does Dad.
They know that I'm a crocodile
and they love me.
I have every right to to do my crocodile thing.

I tell them about my day.
I tell them what I did
and that I didn't eat anybody.

"You are Ivan, my Ivan," mum says,
and takes me in her arms.

Today I'm standing at the **big** classroom window.
I'm keeping watch.

Everyone is sitting down, everyone

except me.

I am a **crocodile**

and I'm watching over the river that flows

through the **m**iddle of the schoolyard.

All of a sudden,
something moves
behind the reeds that line the riverbank.

The teacher doesn't see this.
She is speaking to the children and
the children are listening to her.

But I see it. I see it.

It's a crocodile,
climbing up the riverbank.

Now he's opening his mouth,
he's calling me!

I press my face hard up against the window pane,
scratching the glass with my fingers.

He makes a noise and I do too.
It's a low, throaty growl,
a crocodile growl.

I knock on the window and I call him:
Here I am,
my friend,
here I am.

That **d**oes it,
he sees me.
I keep tapping
on the window **p**ane.

The teacher **t**akes my arm.

"Ivan, dear,
        calm down Ivan, please."

In the yard, the crocodile is turning around,
he's going away, he's **d**iving into the river.

Don't go away yet!
    Come back crocodile.
Friend!
    My friend!

My fingernails scratch the window pane.

Come back!
    Come back ...
        See you tomorrow ...

The teacher calls me.
She's holding a book.

"I have a story for you, **I**van."

I turn my head towards her and I smile,
showing my fine crocodile teeth.

"Are you **C**oming, Ivan?"

I'm coming, Miss!

I run over and take my place,
sitting down amongst the others.

This edition published in 2012 by Berbay Publishing Pty Ltd
English translation © Berbay Publishing Pty Ltd 2012
www.berbaybooks.com
© L'Atelier du Poisson Soluble, 2011
Moi, Ivan Crocodile!, written by René Gouichoux and
illustrated by Julia Neuhaus

English adaptation by Michael Sedunary
Edited by Bryony Oliver-Skuse
Typesetting: Kylie Hall
Printed and bound in China by Everbest Printing
National Library of Australia
Cataloguing-in publication data:
Gouichoux, René
I am Ivan Crocodile!

For primary school children
ISBN 978-0-9806711-3-1